SUPER MONSTERS

A BAD CASE OF THE HICCUPS

Adapted by **SHANNON PENNEY**

SCHOLASTIC INC.

All rights reserved. Published by Scholastic Inc., *Publishers since 1920*. SCHOLASTIC and associated logos are trademarks and/or registered trademarks of Scholastic Inc.

The publisher does not have any control over and does not assume any responsibility for author or third-party websites or their content.

No part of this publication may be reproduced, stored in a retrieval system, or transmitted in any form or by any means, electronic, mechanical, photocopying, recording, or otherwise, without written permission of the publisher. For information regarding permission, write to Scholastic Inc., Attention: Permissions Department, 557 Broadway, New York, NY 10012.

ISBN 978-1-338-35494-2

10 9 8 7 6 5 4 3 2 1   19 20 21 22 23
Printed in the U.S.A.   40

First printing 2019
Book design by Jessica Meltzer

Before Katya finishes her spell . . .

HICCUP!

Katya turns Igor's clothes into funny colors.

Wow!

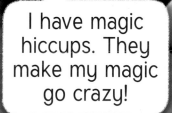

I have magic hiccups. They make my magic go crazy!

HICCUP!

Katya's umbrella lifts Zoe into the air.

Are my magic hiccups gone?

HICCUP! Nope!

Katya's magic gives Zoe a flower crown.

It gives Frankie bouncy springs on his feet!

You should howl at the moon!

You can make funny faces to get rid of hiccups.

Fresh air will blow the hiccups away.

Cleo makes a gust of wind.

Katya makes funny faces and howls.

HICCUP!

No! My magic is still out of control!

23

Now Drac has a red clown nose.

Katya's magic grows a flower under Frankie.

It covers Spike and Zoe in polka dots.

It lifts Cleo in the air.

It brushes Lobo with a feather.

Katya stomps inside.

Sometimes you just need to wait.

OK. I will help you clean up.

28

29

Now I'll try my spell again.

Katya points her wand at the rock.
She says her spell.

The rock turns into a cat toy!

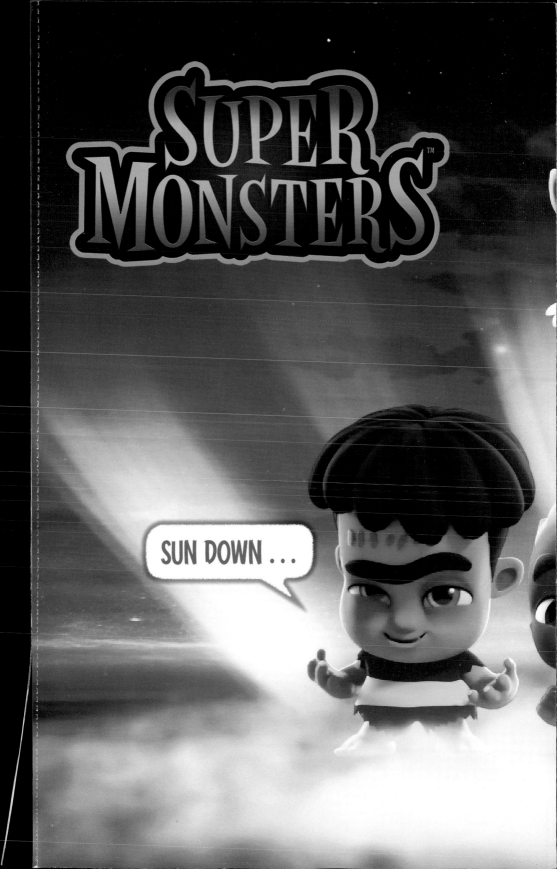